FORT WORTH PUBLIC LIBRARY
W9-BXX-929

THE SCHOOL IS NOT WHITE!

A TRUE STORY OF THE CIVIL RIGHTS MOVEMENT

DOREEN RAPPAPORT illustrated by CURTIS JAMES

JUMP AT THE SUN • HYPERION BOOKS FOR CHILDREN • NEW YORK

In memory of Mae Bertha and Matthew Carter

Printed in Singapore
First Edition
1 3 5 7 9 10 8 6 4 2
This book is set in Mrs. Eaves.
Reinforced binding
Library of Congress Cataloging-in-Publication Data on file.
ISBN 0-7868-1838-7
Visit www.jumpatthesun.com

THIS IS A TRUE STORY about an American family. In 1965, Matthew and Mae Bertha Carter were sharecroppers on a cotton plantation in Mississippi, nine miles from the small town of Drew. Growing cotton is a hard life, and sharecroppers earn very little money. Like all parents, Matthew and Mae Bertha Carter dreamed of a better life for their children. Their children dreamed of better lives, too.

In 1965, seven of the Carters' school-age children attended all-black schools. The schools in Drew were still segregated by race then, even though the U.S. Supreme Court had declared school segregation illegal eleven years before. Like all Southern black schools, theirs were inferior to the white schools in Drew. In August of that year, under a new federal law, the county offered a "freedom of choice" plan for black children to attend any school they wanted. The Carter children signed up to go to the all-white schools. They expected other black families would send their children, too.

RUTH WAS ONLY SIXTEEN,
but she felt tired.
Tired of the hand-me-down readers
and the broken-down school bus
and the patched school roof
and the library that had no books.
She wanted to go to the white school
where everything was crisp and new.
Ruth did not want to end up picking
cotton like Mama and Papa.
Neither did her sisters and brothers.
Her parents agreed.
Mae Bertha and Matthew Carter knew
a good education would get their
children out of the cotton fields.
They signed the papers for them
to go to the all-white school.

Mae Bertha heard the blaring horn
long before she saw the pickup truck.
"It's starting," Matthew said softly.
It was the plantation overseer.
They knew he had come to order them
not to send their children
to the white school.
"I'll help you withdraw them,"
the man said.
"Don't need any help," answered
Matthew.

Mae Bertha smiled to herself
and lugged a chair and record player
out to the porch.
She turned up the volume
and placed the needle gently on a record.
And President John F. Kennedy's voice
blared louder than any truck horn.
"When Americans are sent to war,
we do not ask for whites only.
American students of any color should
be able to attend any school they select
without having to be backed up by troops."

The President's words boomed
as the pickup truck roared away,
leaving only a trail of dust.

That night, rifle shots pierced
the walls and windows of their house.
Matthew and Mae Bertha rocked
their children in their arms
until their trembling bodies
quieted down.
Matthew sat up all night,
a shotgun at his side,
guarding his family.

"We have to show others
it can be done, and maybe
they will stop being afraid,"
Papa said.

They knew he was right.
Dear sweet Papa,
who never wore overalls because
they reminded him of slavery.

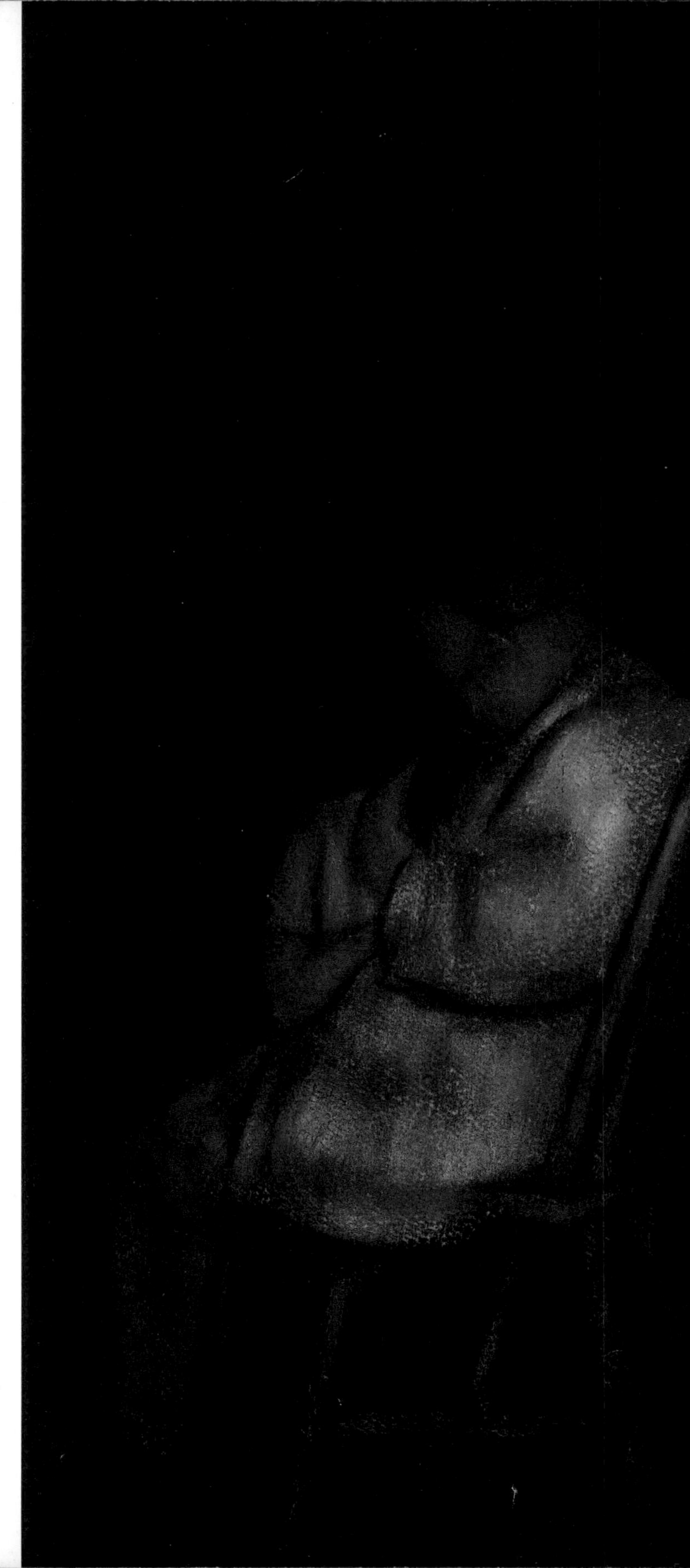

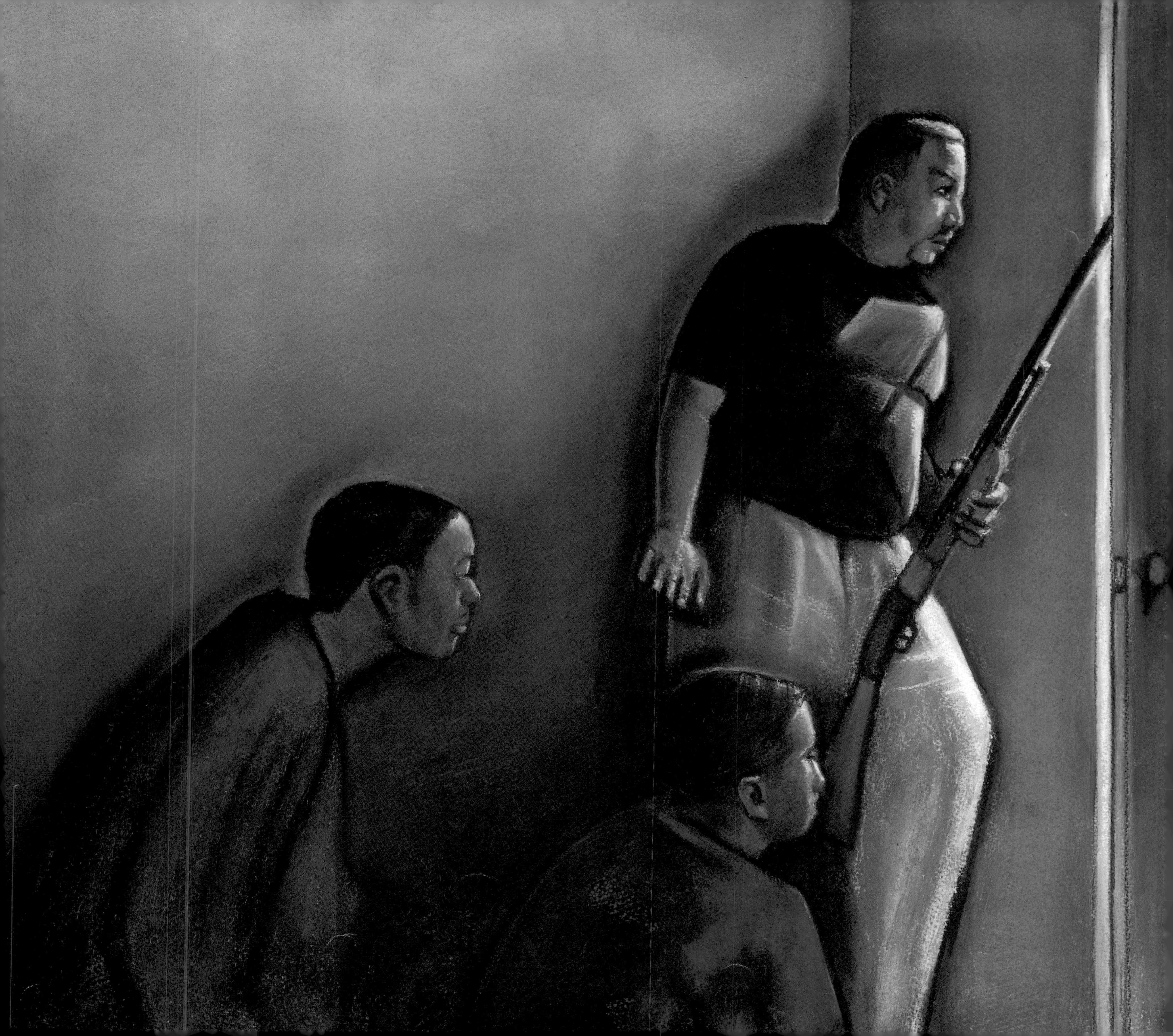

SCHOOL BUS

On September 3, 1965,
Mae Bertha and Matthew Carter
watched their seven children
go off to war
in a shiny yellow school bus.
Four-year-old Carl
stood alongside his parents,
wishing he were old enough to go
with his sisters and brothers.

Sixteen-year-old Ruth,
fifteen-year-old Larry,
thirteen-year-old Stanley,
twelve-year-old Gloria,
ten-year-old Pearl,
eight-year-old Beverly,
six-year-old Deborah—
off to war,
armed only with love.

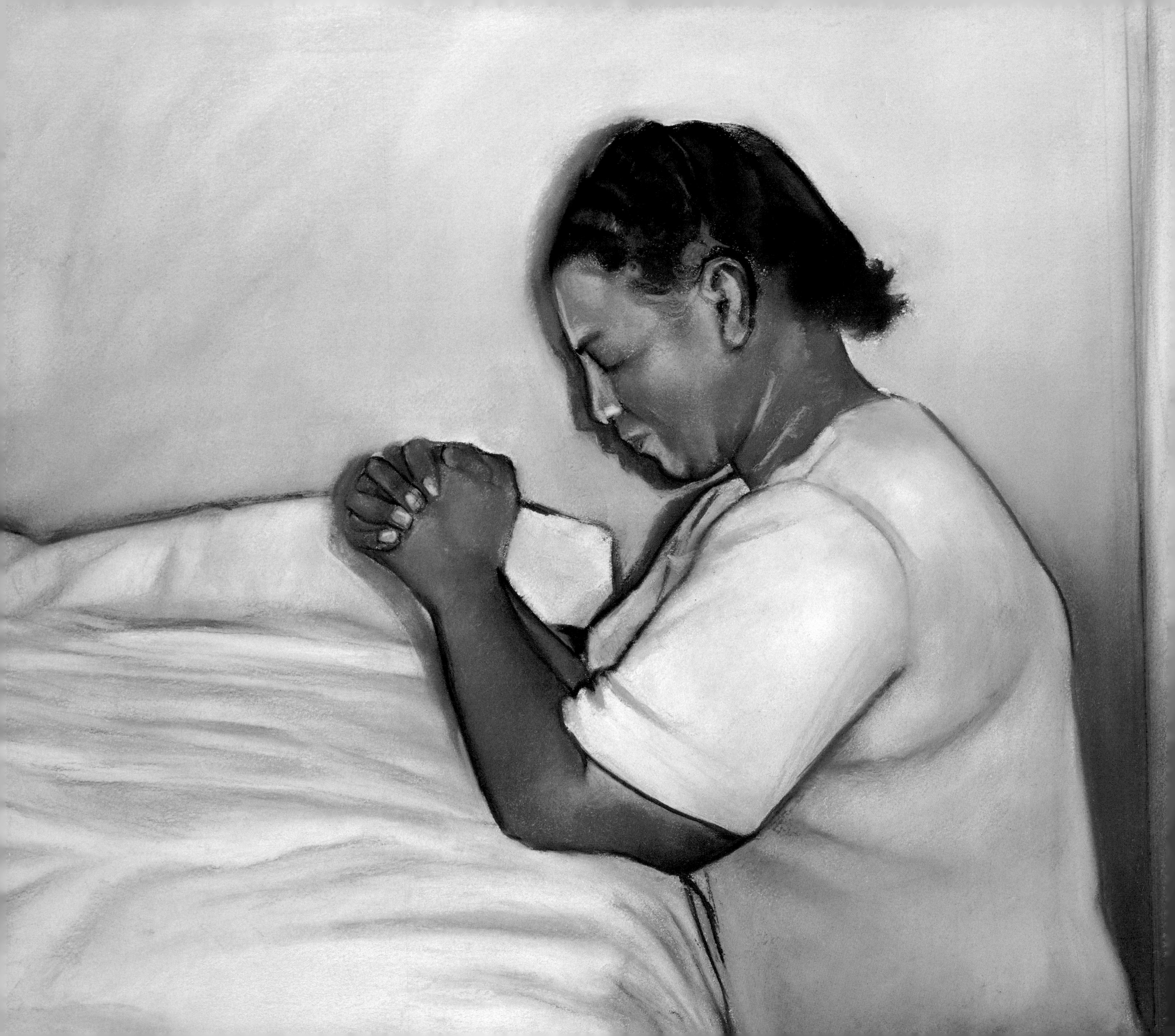

When the bus pulled out of sight,
Matthew went off to the cotton fields.
Mae Bertha, who rarely missed work,
took to her bed and prayed
for God to protect her children.

Mama was waiting on the porch
when the spanking-clean yellow bus
brought them home.
"How did it go today?"
She asked the question
even though she knew the answer.

Mama did not have to hear
the mocking laughter
and the ugly words
to know what had happened that day.

She did not have to see
the angry faces and raised fists
and the spitballs at their heads
and the kicking at their heels
to know what had happened that day.

She knew all too well
that what had happened that day
would happen every day
as long as her children
went to the white school.

She looked into their hurt and angry eyes
and reminded them,
"The school is not white.
It's brown brick.
And that school belongs to you
as well as it belongs to them."
Mama, who left school
at a third-grade level,
was smarter than any white teacher.

The plantation owner came.
He told the family
there would be no cotton to pick
and no house to live in
and no credit at the plantation store
unless they withdrew the children.
They had expected this,
but not so soon.
But for the Carters,
there was no going back.

News of their courage and troubles
reached sympathetic ears.
A Southern black ministry group
and a Northern white church group
sent money for food and clothing.
A Quaker group provided
a down payment for a house.
Civil rights activists found them jobs.
But it was still tough going.

Every school day brought new stories
and more of the same.
Pearl's teacher told her she smelled.
Papa scrubbed her every morning
and washed and ironed her clothes,
so when the teacher said it again,
she would know it was a lie,
even though the lie hurt.

A white girl sometimes spoke to Deborah
when no one else was around.
The principal found out
and told the girl not to.

Whenever they took a seat
in the cafeteria,
their classmates jumped up
as if they were poison.

Ruth and Stanley and Larry
stopped eating lunch,
until Papa found out.

Beverly ate alone on the gym steps
or along the wall outside
and watched her classmates play.

Every day after school Gloria prayed,
"Let tomorrow be an okay day."
But it never was.
Still, she never thought of quitting.

Three years passed,
bringing more ugly words,
mocking laughter,
raised fists, and spitballs.

Carl was now in school.
One day the loneliness choked him,
and his seven-year-old legs marched him
out of school all the way home.
"I'm not going back, Mama."
He crawled into bed.
Mama felt his pain
as if it were hers.
But still she encouraged him to return,
for she and Matthew knew
that Carl's future depended
on education.

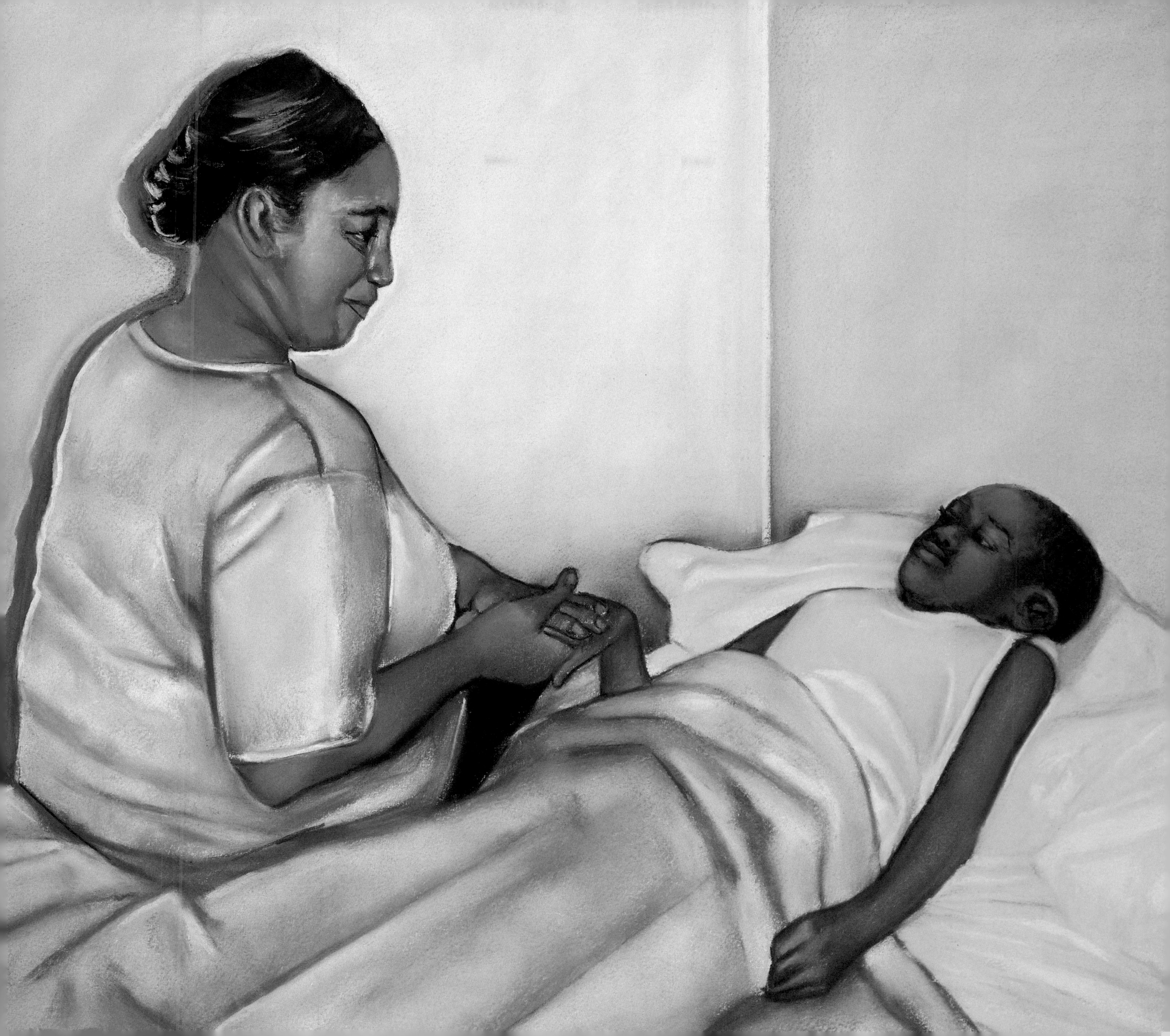

Mae Bertha wrote to the teacher.
She wrote to the principal.
She went to the school.
But no matter how many letters she wrote
or how many visits she made,
nothing changed.

Sometimes Matthew and Mae Bertha's love
could not stop their children's pain
from exploding into hate, and ugly words
spilled from their children's mouths.
Then Mama reminded them
that people who hate cannot feel good.
"Love thine enemy," she quoted
from the Bible.

Every morning
for five years,
the Carter children walked
as straight as tree trunks,
down the gravel road,
carrying books that felt heavier
than any hundred-pound sack of cotton.

SCHOOL

Up the steps, onto the spanking-clean bus
where no one sat next to them.
Past the school yard
where no one played with them.
Into the school where only
unfriendly eyes met theirs.

Down the halls,
into their classrooms,
ignoring the name-calling
and mocking laughter
and raised fists
and the spitballs.
Ignoring it,
but never getting used to it.
Still they stayed on,
hoping to give courage to others,
hoping to make the world a better place.

Gradually, what Papa said would happen
did happen.
Their courage gave courage to
other black families, and black children
signed up for the white schools.
The Carter children knew that
their struggle had made a difference.
And their parents' dream of a better life
for their children came true.

AUTHOR'S NOTE

In 1996, I read a most astounding book, *Silver Rights*, by Constance Curry. It introduced me to the people you have met in this book. There were thirteen Carter children. Five had already graduated from high school by the time the events in this book took place.

Curry was working for the American Friends Service Committee (AFSC), a Quaker organization, at the same time the Carter children were integrating Drew's schools. She met the family while investigating incidents of intimidation and reprisals against black families integrating all-white schools in Mississippi.

The courage, determination, and resiliency of the Carter family in the face of such ugliness and injustice touched me deeply and stayed with me. I had met other "extraordinary ordinary" people in the summer of 1965 when I was teaching in a freedom school in McComb, Mississippi. Their bravery and resolve transformed my life and ideals and set me on the path of writing about people I call "not-yet-celebrated" Americans. While reading Curry's book, I knew this was a story I wanted to tell. It took me many years to find my way of telling it.

All the words spoken by the Carters are as they were reported to Constance Curry. I simplified President Kennedy's speech without distorting its meaning to make it more accessible to young readers. Mae Bertha stayed in school until the seventh grade, but her education was so poor she considered herself as not having been taught beyond a third-grade level.

I remain grateful to Constance Curry for making the Carters' story available to all of us and for her help in assuring its accuracy. I thank Lisa Dicken, Principal, A.W. James Elementary School, Drew, Mississippi, for her help also. I feel honored that the Carter family trusted me with their history. Their present lives prove that Matthew and Mae Bertha's dream of a better life for their children came true.

THE CARTER FAMILY HISTORY

MATTHEW CARTER (1909–1988) and **MAE BERTHA CARTER** (1923–1999)

Matthew and Mae Bertha Carter got their high school equivalency degrees in 1969. Matthew worked for almost twenty years as a teacher's aide in the Ruleville Head Start Program. At his funeral service in 1988, his children offered this eulogy: "You were the dearest, kindest father anyone could ever have. You stood by us when we were in trouble, comforted us when we were in pain, and sympathized with us when we were in sorrow. Your strength will always be remembered, and your love always felt."

MAE BERTHA continued battling for quality education until her death in 1999. In 1982, she received the Wonder Woman Foundation Award in the category of "Women Taking Risks." Her determination and achievement were finally recognized in Mississippi in 1993 when she was chosen as one of six black Mississippians to receive the seventh annual award of distinction.

Mae Bertha and Matthew Carter's dreams for their children came true. The eight children written about in this book graduated from high school; seven graduated from the University of Mississippi; two have advanced degrees. Now adults, they generously share their dreams with us.

RUTH CARTER WHITTLE b. 1949–

For 29 years Ruth has worked with special-needs children in Toledo, Ohio. She has two children: Ngina, 33, and Tandra, 25; and two grandchildren, Jade, 12, and Taylor, 10.

> *My parents had great expectations for their children. I don't think my dreams for my children could be any better. When I was little, I dreamed of living in a house with indoor plumbing, a telephone, and a store close by where I could buy ice cream. I have that. Now I would like to have a big house with a country kitchen. I would also like to write my own book and be on television talking about it.*

LARRY CARTER b. 1950–

After a 20-year career in the U.S. Air Force, Larry works for the Virginia Department of Social Services, establishing paternity for children and collecting child support from noncustodial parents. Larry and his wife, Chong, have two children, Shawnee, 24, and Darren, 22.

> *We still face some of the same challenges of discrimination today as we did back in the sixties, so the dreams that I have for my children are the same as the dreams my parents had for me. When I was a child, we were separated by race. Now we are separated by income and race. Since my children are biracial, they face prejudice, even from within their own races. My dream is to continue to assist my children in becoming self-sufficient adults.*

STANLEY CARTER b. 1952–

Stanley works for Sunoco Logistics in Tulsa, Oklahoma, as a scheduler for the Oil Movements Group. He and his wife, Carrie, have a 36-year-old daughter, Marci, and a 19-year-old son, Stan.

> *My parents wanted a good education for all of their children. That's also what I want for mine. I still dream of visiting Africa, the birthplace of our ancestors. Maybe one day it will happen.*

GLORIA DICKERSON b. 1953–

Gloria is a certified public accountant with a master's degree in business administration. After eighteen years in the Job Corps, she is the controller at the Kellogg Foundation. She and her husband, Donald, have a 32-year-old son, Deidrick.

> *I have some of the same dreams for my son as my parents had for me. I want him to be educated, self-sufficient, and happy. I want him to have a wonderful family and to enjoy life to the fullest. I have been able to overcome poverty. Now I am ready to give back. For me personally, I would love to be an advocate and voice for people in the Mississippi Delta who need help improving their quality of life.*

PEARL CARTER OWENS b. 1955–

Pearl manages the Oxford, Mississippi, office of a crude-oil pipeline company. She and her husband, Raymond, have four children: LaToya Green, 25; Davin Owens, 22; Jason Green, 22; and Jeremy Owens, 20, and granddaughter K'myua Green, 3.

> *I passed on my parents' dreams for me to my children—to acquire a good education and to be able always to depend on themselves. I myself have always wanted to go to home-interior–decorating school and still think about it.*

BEVERLY CARTER b. 1957–

Beverly has a master's degree in elementary education and teaches second grade in Fayetteville, Georgia. She has three children: Brittany, 5; Shayla, 20; and Kerry, 24.

> *My parents wanted me to live a happy and successful life filled with great times and few hardships. This is all I want for my own children. Like my mother, I also know that this will only happen if my children are well educated. My personal dream is to be the best teacher I can be. I want to have a great impact on my students' lives. I want to be remembered as a wonderful teacher, a legend.*

DEBORAH CARTER SMITH b. 1959–

Deborah is an accountant at the University of Mississippi. She and her husband, James, have two sons: James Jr., 18, and Jarryl, 16.

> *Like my parents hoped for me, I hope my children will receive the best possible education and lead happy and productive lives. My continued wish is to travel and see more of the world. I would love to travel to Africa and see some of the places where slaves were held before they were shipped to the United States.*

CARL CARTER b. 1961–

Carl is the Director of Material Management for Baptist Memorial Hospital in Columbus, Mississippi. Carl and his wife, Upea, have two children: Kutee, 25, and Bryan, 14.

> *My parents wanted us to be well educated and prepared to handle the challenges that life bestows on us. I want the same for my kids. For myself, I want to continue to grow spiritually.*

IF YOU WANT TO LEARN MORE ABOUT THE LIVES OF BLACK CHILDREN IN THE SOUTH FROM THE EARLY TWENTIETH CENTURY THROUGH THE CIVIL RIGHTS MOVEMENT, READ:

Bridges, Ruby. *Through My Eyes.* New York: Scholastic, Inc., 1999.

Curry, Constance. *Silver Rights.* San Diego: Harvest Books, 1996.

Greenfield, Eloise, and Lessie Jones Little. *Childtimes.* New York: Thomas Y. Crowell, 1996.

King, Casey, and Linda Barrett Osborne. *Oh, Freedom!: Kids Talk About the Civil Rights Movement with the People Who Made It Happen.* Minneapolis: Sagebrush Education Resources, 1997.

Levine, Ellen. *Freedom's Children.* New York: Putnam Juvenile, 2000.

Parks, Rosa, and James Haskins. *I Am Rosa Parks.* New York: Puffin Books, 1999.

Taylor, Mildred D. *The Friendship.* Illustrated by Max Ginsburg. New York: Puffin Books, 1998.

Wiles, Deborah. *Freedom Summer.* New York: Simon & Schuster Children, 2001.